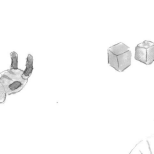

For William

Little Bean's Friend
Text and illustrations copyright © 1996 by John Wallace.
First published in Great Britain by HarperCollins Publishers Ltd.
First American edition, 1997. HarperCollins®, ☀®, and HarperFestival® are trademarks of HarperCollins Publishers Inc. Printed in Hong Kong. All rights reserved.

Little Bean's
Friend

John Wallace

📚 HarperFestival®
A Division of HarperCollinsPublishers

Little Bean and Bouncer played inside.

"Little Bean! You're making far too much noise!"

"That's enough.
Time to play outside, both of you."

"It's a beautiful day. You'll have more fun
in the yard."

Little Bean changed into her swimsuit
and ran outside.

Little Bean slid
down the slide.

She climbed
in the playhouse.

She dug
in the sandbox

and sprayed
the garden hose.

She rode
her tricycle

and splashed
in the pool.

When the sun went in,
Little Bean changed back into her clothes.

Then she and Bouncer ran
around and around

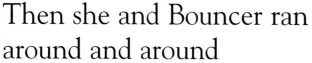

and played tag until…

she got so excited she lost her favorite bear.

Little Bean didn't know how to get it back.

"Is this yours?"

Little Bean didn't know what to say.

She ran inside to get her daddy.

"Don't be afraid, Little Bean.
It's only that nice Paul from next door.

Why don't you pop over and say hello?"

"Hello, Nice Paul. I'm Little Bean.
Do you want to play?"

They slid
down the slide

and climbed
in the playhouse.

They dug
in the sandbox

and sprayed the garden hose.

They rode
Little Bean's tricycle

and splashed
in the pool.

"Nice Paul, will you be my friend again tomorrow?"